By Rayne Havok

For Jeffery Dahmer, who taught me it's ok to have fucked up thoughts, so long as you don't act on them, and to write them instead.

Summary

Xavier: "I escaped from prison, hauling ass in a stolen car, putting space between me and that barbed wire fence, when the damn thing runs out of gas.

Luckily, I come across an old farmhouse that looks empty, even luckier, it is not.

The threats about daddy coming home don't scare me... maybe they should have

Warning

I'm told this book should have an 'extreme' warning.

Because these things are always in my head and on my mind, I don't always consider them to be over- the- top. To some it may be run- of- the mill and to others it may be too much.

If you feel like you may have issues reading 'extreme' stories please do not bother with this one, you may be offended.

I do not condone any of this shit in real life, please remember this is a work of fiction and as always do not try this at home.

Chapter 1

The gas light had just come on, I figured I had a few more miles to look for a station, but that's the thing, when you steal a car you don't really know all the ins and outs of its mechanics. This one seems to have a malfunctioning gas gauge.

Fucking thing leaves me stranded on the side of some shithole road with nothing in sight but trees on either side. I haven't seen another car in a hundred miles. The hour of night doesn't help, 1:00 am– I shouldn't expect much.

I've been hauling ass through this town and now I'm trapped inside of it until I can figure something else out. I need to find a place to hunker down, hopefully get some shut- eye so I can do this all again tomorrow. I need even more miles between me and the high walls of that fucking prison.

I choose a path that looks the easiest to hike through and go into the forested area. It's a cool night and the breeze is refreshing. I can't see anything in front of me but the trees, tons and tons of fucking trees, what a shitty spot to get stranded.

I have been walking for what feels like miles, but really it can't be, it's the terrain that makes it feel that long. I trip again and catch myself before I fall another time– I am getting really irritated by this shit.

I look up to survey my options now, thinking I may just save myself a broken ankle and crash here for the night, when a glint from the moon's reflection catches my eye and I thank my fucking luck that something is here.

I can make out the rest of the window and as I walk closer, the rest of the farmhouse comes into view. It's an old run down building that looks at least a hundred years old. A wrap around porch that's missing most of the banister, shutters hanging on by the skin of their teeth, and the siding dirty and dilapidated.

I can't imagine it's occupied, but I walk carefully around it to investigate the likelihood. I can't see anything that alarms me so, I grab a rock and knock it against one of the small panes of glass near the door. I spend a full minute listening before reaching my hand in to find the lock.

The door creaks as I push it slowly inward. The kitchen is right inside and from what I can see of it, it's dirty and dusty, looks like no one has cared about it for some time.

I'm riffling through the cupboards to find some none perishables when movement catches my eye, and for fuck sake, it couldn't be a more welcoming site. I move my head slowly in the direction of the girl in the white top– I say that only because it's the only thing she's wearing, well, that and a tiny pair of pink panties. I can't take my eyes from that little V of fabric.

It's been so long since I've been in the presence of a young woman– *any* woman actually, and my god, she is young. She looks fresh out of high school. My blood is instantly hot, my cock so hard it could push through the zipper on my jeans.

"What are you doing in here?" she says in a sleepy voice. I probably woke her breaking the window.

I creep forward slowly, so as not to alarm her, "I got turned around out there, I thought this place was empty." I slow my pace even more, creeping like a hunting cat might do, and inch by inch, my feet get closer to her. "Is there someone here that could help me?"

She shakes her head.

I can't imagine this girl is alone out here all by herself. "Your parents aren't here?" I'm almost close enough to grab her now. I can smell her sweet scent, something floral, and it is calling to me.

"My mom is asleep; I can go get her if you want." Her voice is full of innocence– just what I like.

"No, sugar, you don't need to do that." I reach out quickly, seizing my opportunity, one arm wraps around her small waist and the other tightens over her mouth. She tries to get free, but I lift her up and keep her from being able to run. It doesn't stop her legs from flailing about, kicking wildly in the struggle.

Her back is pressed to my front and she's squirming against me, rubbing her little ass against my cock. I almost can't breathe, it's been so long for me.

Eight years in the Pen, with each day feeling like a hundred, eight fucking years without a woman– this poor little girl doesn't know what she's doing to

me right know, how she is driving me wild with her struggle.

I've been a 'free' man for nine hours, most of which were spent jacking a car and fleeing from police who gave chase for a while until I could evade them. No time really, to enjoy my freedom, yet. And this little lady is just ripe for the picking.

I look frantically for somewhere to take her, somewhere, that if she makes noise, she won't be heard so easily. "Stop squirming, little girl." My voice is raspy with lust. My grip tightens around her, trying to calm her movements but it only makes her struggle more. "Oh, fuck." I lose it, I fucking come right in my pants. I grind my cock into her ass, jerking the rest of my release.

I think she knows what just happened because she stills. I wish she would have done that when I asked her to before so I wouldn't have to walk around with this load in my jeans, but I'm grateful either way, it's made it easier to haul her around.

The house is dark, but my luck holds true, and I am able to find a spot for her. I push open the last door and it is a bedroom– looks like it hasn't been used in long time. The bed is a welcome sight. My mind becomes a kaleidoscope of depraved images with her being the star.

I plop her on top of the comforter and the dust dances in the moon light. I cover my mouth to avoid choking; giving her the time she needed to squirm off the bed. I grab her by the hair and rip her back toward me. She yelps and goes stick straight from the pain. The tiny tears pricking her eyes feed right into me– I want more of those.

I get her back onto the bed, using the weight of my own body to hold her down; then I sit on top of her and straddle her waist, ripping open her tee- shirt. Her round, young tits are beautiful, but before I let myself become too distracted by them, I make long strips from the torn shirt and restrain her with them, wrapping them tightly around her wrists and through the slats in the bedframe, immobilizing her.

I wrap a thick one around her mouth, securing it tightly behind her head. It muffles her enough that I don't worry about the noise she might make. The house is huge, and from what I've seen of the bottom floor, no one else is near.

I shimmy down her body. God, it's been so long since I've smelled a woman, I bury my nose into her panties and breathe in her scent. I get so fucking hard, harder than I thought possible, my adolescent cock has nothing on me now.

The last woman I had was on my last night as a free man, a saggy- titted- fatty that I caught while she was getting into her vehicle; I fucked her in the backseat of her minivan. She wasn't even worth it, just another tally to add to my list. She had some panic button she was able to push to alert the cops. I was zipping back up when I heard the sirens approaching quickly. No time to run, they were on me in seconds, cuffing me and tossing me into the back of a squad car.

I went down for the string of rapes that they were able to tie me to after getting my DNA. They'd

said I was an atrocious monster for what I did to all those girls. Photo after photo of all the woman who'd come forward for my trial. Their little snatches all scared up and on display for everyone in the courtroom to see, some photos of the fresh cuts crisscrossing on top of their pussies coming from the ones who ran to the emergency room to get a rape- kit done right away.

I had been at it for years before being caught; there were a lot of woman I marked with my X, that's what I've always been called, X, it's short for Xavier. These bitches should have been proud to wear my name etched into their skin, a constant reminder of being chosen. Instead, were sending me off to a lifetime in prison.

The jury threw the book at me, and with twenty- seven confirmed cases of mutilation and violent rape I wasn't surprised. What did surprise me was the small amount that had come forward. I always knew not every woman came forward after a rape, what I didn't know is that number is huge. I should have had one hundred and eighteen, by my

count– and I *did* count. That's exactly how many woman I'd raped at that point– all bearing my X– all my whores. An overwhelming majority must have been satisfied with our time together since I didn't see them at the trail complaining.

My first notch being an old woman in the neighborhood who asked me for help in her yard, which was commonplace in a neighborhood like the one mine was growing up. You helped each other out. And I helped myself to her. I was young and inexperienced– it was over quickly. I'm surprised still, to this day, that she didn't rat me out, she knew who my mom was and could've just told her, I actually waited for them to haul me off to jail for it. But, the days past and nothing ever came of it. The worst that happened was I was never invited to help with work for her again– not a punishment, if you ask me.

Although, it wasn't as gruesome as the later ones she did still have my mark crudely engraved into her fleshy old woman mound.

I had finished with the work and she offered me a lemonade, I took it from her graciously, the woman's chores had worked me into a sweat, sipping it and talking to her, my eyes wandering to her fleshy thighs. I lost all restraint and my compulsion took over. I took the knife she had used to cut a piece of pie for herself and I put it to her throat. Before I knew what I was doing, I had my virgin dick inside of her, I had nothing to compare it to and it felt so good. It took only a minute before I exploded in her, the second minute past and I was rocking inside of her again.

The knife got lost for a moment, and before I knew it, I had cut her. A long jagged slice right on the top of her hairy pussy, the blood lubricated us, excited me, and while I fucked her, I cut across that line and made an X, marking her for me.

The only sounds she had made were the cries from being cut, other than that, she was silent and unmoving. I finished inside of her a second time with a mixture of her blood and my come oozing from her hole. From that day on I knew what I needed. And by

not going to police she helped me do it to four more woman that summer before my senior year.

I had served eight full fucking years of my sentence before exacting my escape. It had been a plan in the making since day one. Now, I'm a 35-year- old man getting back on the horse, so to speak— if by horse you mean hot, young, piece of ass. This girl will be a 'welcome back to the real world' prize. I'm practically salivating with lust as I touch her.

Chapter 2

I run my fingers up and down her tight little body, firm in all the right places, juicy in the others. It's been a long time since I've touched something so smooth.

I cut away her panties with the pocket- knife I found in the hot- wired car and spread her legs apart. The smell of her hits me again, young and fresh. I push my fingers into her tight hole and it barely gives at all, she is so fucking tight. I pull my fingers out to taste her– so sweet it makes me lightheaded.

I get rid of my pants and shirt, tossing them onto the floor then come back to her. Pressing her knees to her chest I bury my face in her pussy, licking and tasting her, sucking her tiny little clit into my mouth I eat her pussy like a ferocious mad man.

She squirms around but is unable to escape my firm hold on her. I know from experience I can make a girl come against her will and I feel her on the verge, driving me wild with control, I taste the warm juice that seeps out of her as she quivers under my tongue.

"Good girl, making it all wet for me." She hides her face against her arm, shamefully.

I lap up all that goodness and slip my fingers back into her, it slides freely now as I push it deeper inside of her.

I can't stand not being in her another second and I want to feel her stretching. I push my cock into her. Her eyes go wide as the pain of my large shaft tears into her.

I thrust into her with no regard for her pain, my balls slap against her ass. I jackhammer her until I feel myself getting close, only then do I ease up and move with a little less vigor. I push in and pull out slowly, letting her tightness milk me. Then, when I can't hold back another second, I release my load inside of her, collapsing onto her chest, completely and utterly spent.

I take her nipple into my mouth and suck it like a hungry baby; each pull contracts her hole, tightening around my cock. I bite down hard, tasting her blood, stopping only when my teeth meet. I tear the nub away from her breast and spit it onto the floor, and she cries and struggles under me.

Fear envelopes her face, she knows now that I am a *real* monster. I smear her blood across her chest and take her throat into my hand. She stops breathing right away, and still I squeeze harder, she frantically starts kicking and it has the desired effect, I let her struggling movements work my cock. She begins to fade, her body not able to move without oxygen in the brain, I release her and her nose starts drawing in air as she struggles to get it back.

I flip her over, twisting her arms painfully above her head then pull her up onto her knees with her asshole pointed right at me. I push into it, tearing it open. I have to catch my breath; my excitement is overflowing my lungs.

When I regain control of my own breathing, my shaking hands grip her by the waist and I fuck her. Using her hips, I push and pull her away from me as I watch my cock disappear into her hole.

I smack her ass and her roundness jiggles. God, it looks so good. I hit her repeatedly until her ass is on fire, heat from my palm's marks radiate. I

tug her harder and faster, excited to unload in her back hole. I come loudly, grunting like an animal.

I hear a loud crack and she screams through her gag. I don't stop to investigate what might have broken, I'm too caught up in the aftermath of my much needed release.

I twist her back over, she lets out another scream, and I know it must have been her shoulder that had snapped. I put her legs together and sit on top of her knees to hold her in place while I carve my X into her, it's deeper than I usually do them, but I want this one to stand out.

I saw during the trial that some of them had faded. I want this one with her forever, I stab into her and slide along her skin, an inch or so deep, until the letter is gushing like a geyser, pulsing between her legs. I slip my finger inside the X, up to the first knuckle, and then I trace it.

That one is going to look good forever.

I leave her tied up tightly and go in search of her mother whom she said was home. She may not be

as young and hot as her daughter, but I still want a go of her.

Chapter 3

I pull my jeans back up, not bothering to zip them, and head back out in the direction I came, passing the kitchen as I go, I grab a glass and fill it with water from the tap. I'm so thirsty from that work out.

There is a huge staircase in the center of the living room, it has about eight steps and then a landing that forks off and goes in either direction with another eight steps, or so. I choose left and ascend to the top. I don't hear any noise, so I sneak quietly with my hand along the wall for guidance. There is a long hallway with many doors; I open them all as I pass, making sure to clear each one. The second is a bathroom and I take the opportunity to empty my bladder.

The next, and last door, is a bedroom; a nightlight helps aid in my investigation of the room. There is a girl sleeping, not the mother as I was expecting, but a girl to be about the age of the other one. It's hard to tell with people just how old they are, and if you ask me, if they have titties and a little hair on their pussies, they're legal.

She is blonde and small; I can hear her breathing, slowly in and out. I look at all the things she has decorating her room with, getting a better feel for the sleeping beauty in the bed.

Trophies line the walls on shelves made to display them all. I read one and it tells me she is a gymnast, which may explain her slight frame. She's won over a hundred of these by my estimated count. Her high school diploma framed along with other certificates she must be proud of.

Her name is Eliza by the name printed on everything.

She stirs in her bed, her white lacy cover gets tangled in her legs, pulling the blanket down a bit, she's wearing a little, lose fitting, yellow tank top and one of her tits is hanging out. Small little pink buds, only big enough to be called 'puffies' making my mouth water.

I let my pants fall and tug my cock a few times to alleviate the ache before walking over to her and ripping the covers away from her. I hold my hand over her mouth then I grab both of her wrists and lie down on top of her warm- from- sleep body. I pull that little titty into my mouth, licking around in circles and sucking it hard.

Her eyes are wild– as they should be, a naked man lying on top of you as you wake is something that would freak anyone out.

I do the same to the other, leaving both breasts wet and glistening from my saliva, then I pick her up out of her bed and carry her around with me as I go in search of restraints. I really should have done this a minute before, but I was too caught up in the sight of her. I could just overpower her and take what I want, but I know mommy is around here somewhere and I can't alert her.

I find duct tape on her desk, it's cutesy with little ducks on it and nothing seems more fitting than tying her up with it. I pull a strip off with my teeth and fix it to her mouth then move her hands behind her back and wrap them with the tape.

I stand her on her feet and pull her top hard until it stretches and tears, she's shaking so hard her legs can hardly hold her up. She is saying something behind the tape but I don't care to listen or try and understand it.

She is wearing a lacey yellow thong to match her top; I can see she has a bush hiding inside. I press my hand against it and feel her heat right away.

"I'm gonna fuck this hot little twat of yours."

The fear in her eyes makes me hungry; I want to dig right into her. I push her back onto the bed with her hands trapped underneath her. I tug her panties down and get a close look at her warm hole, tickling it with my finger before inserting it.

She shakes her head back and forth wildly and I know why, she's never had anything in this hole. It's the tightest entrance I've ever felt, and my god, I want nothing more than to rip right into it. I want to tear her wide open and watch her bleed.

I tug a few times at my cock and the fear in her eyes almost has me coming already, she is dry as a bone inside her hole but I don't do anything to help her out, I know when I get inside and tear that little membrane the blood will do all the lubricating I need.

I line my hard cock up and I push hard until I fill her hole, I hiss as it grabs tightly and sucks my

I push my finger inside and wiggle it around; stretching her ripped hole, the tears streaming down her face are exhilarating, I love it when the bitches cry.

I lick her sweet and tangy flavor from my finger and then spread her pussy wide and slap it hard with my other hand. The sound reverberates throughout the room; I hit her repeatedly– harder and harder each time, swelling her lips to twice the size.

Her meaty pussy looks hungry now as I push my fingers inside her hole. But the overwhelming need to bury inside of her takes over and I step back and lower her slightly so I get the right angle to do just that. I force my way into her again, and this time, I fuck her wildly until I come. Thrusting relentlessly into her from this angle hurts her; I can tell she is in severe pain. I'm pounding hard into her cervix and it's fresh blood I see, mixed with my come when I pull out of her.

"Poor little girl, so much blood down here, but I want more. Just say the word and I'll stop though." I pause. "Nothing to say, there? Ok, here we go, then."

Not giving her the ability to speak has worked in my favor, I gave her the chance to talk her way out of this, but the tape prevented it, so I guess I get to play all I want with her.

I let her ass fall to the bed and she remains in her pretzel shape, when I get back to her, the cocktail of fluid inside of her spills over and runs down her asshole. I rub it into that hole and push my finger inside to feed it.

I pull out of it and get back on task, reaching for the item I brought over; I show it to her– the latest trophy she'd won. It has a gold figure on the top doing a handstand, its large– looks like a first place winner.

I pull her back onto my thighs, same position I enjoyed a minute ago, and I push the feet of the gymnast into her pussy. She tries to speak, frantically squirming to get away, but at less than a hundred pounds, there's no way she's getting anywhere. I push the figurine into her until it disappears, having to shove harder toward the end as I reach the depths of her, and I fuck her with it hard, cramming it inside of

her with my fist tightly around the base of the trophy with a stabbing motion.

Blood is pouring from her, as I am sure I've demolished her insides. When I feel like I've had enough fun with her, and the ache in my arm tells me to stop, I take the little trophy girl out of her and show her the bloodied figurine. She cries and cries, choking and struggling to breathe through her nose.

There are chunks of her insides caught a part of the trophy. I really ripped her apart, I feel proud knowing I did such a thorough job on her.

Hey, don't judge me, we all need to find pride somewhere in our lives. Me– I find it in the depths of a woman's pussy, bleeding and torn.

I carve my X into her so she can see she gets to wear my mark as her sister does. It is a little harder to manage as her hairs get in the way. It's been a very long time since I've had to deal with such an issue, even when I was doing this eight years ago it wasn't common place to have such a hairy obstacle.

It looks good in the end and I'm sure it will heal nicely... for me. Not so much for her, it will look horrid for her, a constant reminder of what I took from her. And to be completely honest I love when those women think about me, I love knowing I'm in their minds every time they fuck, knowing that even when their sex is consensual, it will trigger thoughts of me. I fucking *thrive* on that.

I leave her on her bed and click the door behind her; I need to find the girls' mom. I don't know if I'll have any nut left for her without becoming dehydrated, but a man's gotta try.

Chapter 4

I go to the other side of the house, passing across the giant staircase in search of dear mommy's room. Another few doors checked before I come to hers, left ajar, probably to hear if there is an intruder

during the night. Not at all effective if that is the truth.

I sneak through the doorway; she is asleep in her bed, facing away from the door. I took the duct tape from little Eliza's room in case– mom is probably bigger and stronger than her little girls are.

I can see that she is a slight woman, blonde hair like her kids'. I take inventory of the room; it is certainly a feminine atmosphere, fresh cut flowers on each of the tops of tables. Floral coverings on her bed, she is sleeping in some pink nighty, long sleeved and ruffled.

Dear god, I hope she's not one of those 'old' moms, I'd hate to finish the night with that.

I pounce on her before she can learn that I am here. She squirms and struggles right away. I flip her onto her back and my god; she has the biggest tits, they're round and plump. I hadn't realized I was missing a set of giant tits until I saw hers. They jiggle as she struggles, and I don't try and calm her, the

effect is working perfectly to get me in the mood again.

When she calms down enough, I chance a look at her face, she is beautiful, and the youthfulness of her daughters' comes through right away.

She's breathing heavy when she tells me, "don't hurt my girl's please. Do whatever you want to me, I won't fight you, but please don't hurt them."

"Oh, honey, let me just say that the little gymnast one nearly sucked my soul through my cock." I lean in and whisper into her ear, "so fucking tight." I rip a piece of tape off and wrap it around her wrists. "Well… not anymore."

The horror of my words hit her and her face contorts as she cries, feeling the pain my words cause her heart.

I finish securing her wrists, pulling them up and over her head, wrapping the tape around the headboard.

"My husband is going to be here soon," she tries.

"I'm not falling for that." There's no way a man lives here, everything screams 'single woman' around here. I flick my knife open and she squeals.

"Please don't hurt me, do whatever you came here for and then leave. Please, you don't have to use that." Her eyes don't leave my weapon.

I push the blade through the fabric of her nighty and slide it all the way down until she is bared to me, her tits looking even better uncovered, no panties to hide her cleanly shaven pussy. Her trim waist and flared hips turn me on. My cock fills out and I'm rock hard for her.

I run my hands up and down her body, "Fuck, woman, you feel *real* good."

I sit back onto her legs and stroke myself, the crusted blood from her daughter flakes off onto her tummy. I take both her big tits in my hand and massage them, squeezing and tugging, they're soft and firm at the same time.

I touch my cock to the center of them and squeeze her tits together to grip my dick. "Please, just be gentle with me."

The innocent look in her eyes feeds my sicko. I dig my nails into her flesh and squeeze harder still, pushing my cock between the pillow-y softness as I fuck her tits, ramming my cock into her neck as I do.

She's crying and the crescent shaped marks on her tits are losing blood, slowly dripping down her skin. I build my momentum, and fuck her like I know she wants me to, then I grab her hair to hold her in place as I spray whatever come my body has remade across her face, then run my fingers through it to paint her with it. "Stick your tongue out."

She does as she is told after I tug at her hair. I brush my come- covered finger against it and make her taste me. "Close it."

She pulls her tongue back in her mouth, fresh tears in her eyes. I don't take offence to them, in fact, I relish the sight of them. They mean I've done my job here.

I ease down the length of her body, and pull her legs apart. "I really want to see if that made you wet. I've been doing this a long time; you wouldn't be the first."

"You don't have time for this, please just go, my husband will be here soon. Please." She's grasping at anything to get me to leave, it only makes me more eager to play.

"Shut up." I lean my weight onto the backs of her thighs, pinning them to her chest, effectively giving me the best view of my target. I check her like a dipstick, in and then out. "Not as wet as I'd like, but for sure, wetter than both your girls were before I made them bleed. I guess being stuck out here in, in the middle of nowhere, would keep most girls virgins."

She's not as flexible as the second girl, Eliza, and I have to struggle to keep her legs out of the way as I push into her hole. I add finger after finger until I'm forcing my fist inside of her, punching into her hard and fast. She is crying, tears streaming down her

cheeks and collecting in her hair, tormented by my hand.

"Please... please... please." She is sobbing and snoting all over; her face is covered in wet.

Her pussy is making all sorts of sloshing noises; it feeds my need to continue. "You're getting wetter now, you hear that. You want to come? I could let you come." I slow my pace in and out, letting her feel my hand inch by inch.

"Please just stop, I don't want this, please. He is coming, you'll regret this– all of this," she says in between her fit.

I rub her little clit gently at first until I feel it twitching. Moving in a rhythm along with my fisted hand, I manipulate her pussy to make her come. But more time passes, and each time I think this will be it, she stops it from happening. She won't let herself come. She's trying hard not to give me the satisfaction.

"I got your daughter off; she came so hard for me."

I knew those words would push her even further from the brink and I don't care, I hate her a little for not letting me win, for have such willpower to deny herself the orgasm.

I draw out my fist completely, but before she can recover, I slam it back into her with all my strength. She yelps in pain but I don't stop, I push and push into the barricade of her hole, trying to shove past it.

I get inside deeper than I've ever felt, pull out my bloody hand, then smack it across her face. Blood pours out of her, as I'm sure I've ruptured something in there, but still, I have things to do to her so I don't let her rest.

I dig my knife into her flesh and give her a matching X to that of her sweet girls– the night of the 'triple X', it will be my most prolific attack. I cut the tape away from the bed and drag her with me down the stairs to the bottom where I reaffix her hands, this time to the banister.

"You stay here, or I will do many more awful things to your girls."

I jog down the stairs to the first ones room and shove her toward her mother, who takes one look at her and sobs, her bloody tit is probably what does it for poor mom.

"One more," I say, coming back with the second one, my favorite little gymnast, Eliza. I found her in her room on top of a puddle of blood oozing from between her legs. I carry her to the first landing and then nudge her forward with my foot hard enough to send her down the second flight of stairs. She rolls down comically, as she is still in the pretzel shape, with her legs secured behind her head.

I pick her up off the floor and show her mother the mutilated hole I have given her, looking even more heinous than when I left her.

"My baby, I'm so sorry, honey." She cries and cries while I affix her daughter to the hand railing beside her.

I have all of them on their knees one on each step next to each other. Naked asses pointed right at me.

"Now, I'd like to play a little game."

"My dad is coming back; he is going to fuck you up." This from the first girl I took.

"Oh, sure honey." I do enjoy her gusto, but I can't believe a word she says, I've heard threats of this sort countless times before– so very unoriginal.

I don't care what these idiot bitches say, I'm going to have my fun with them, and when I leave, it will be because I'm ready to fucking go, and not a second earlier.

"Well, Miss Mouth, you can go first, this is a little game I like to call 'guess what the big bad man is shoving inside of me' you all are going to love it." I'm the only one laughing, which is how I like it.

I take the first object and insert it into her pussy, not too hard– I don't want to kill them, this I'd just for fun, I'm not a murderer, then fuck her with it. She cries as I may have taken too may liberties with

it, blood spills, running down her legs. She doesn't say a word, doesn't even *try* to make a guess. I give it one more hard shove and lean over her to put my mouth next to her ear. "It's the fire poker. You like it?" Nothing from her.

"Ok, since little Eliza took her trophy up her hole, I guess we can move on to mom to complete the first round."

I push the object into her and she cries out immediately as it slices into her swollen hole. "You recognize it don't you?" I pull it out and push it back into her slowly. "I figured you would know one of your own kitchen knives." I take it out of her, slicing along her opening. "Not so tough now, huh? Look how wet I made you from that." I guess I was still holding a grudge against her for not playing my orgasm game. I slide the blade upward as I remove it from her, cutting the small tissue between holes widening her for my next round.

All this blood has effectively refueled me and before I can get on with the game I give the little gymnast another go at my cock, so wet inside that my

cock slips right in, I can't even tell that I'd stretched her at all, she's still so much tighter than the others.

I let them watch if they want, but I don't make them. I grab tightly to the small girls hips and go frantically at her until I unload inside of her, grunting loudly as I come hard.

"God, you ladies sure do know how to make a man feel good." I wipe sweat from my forehead and take a minute to catch my breath. "You know, I might have to take this one with me." I say about Eliza. She could be a lot of fun for a while, and if I can get back to the group, I'm sure a lot of them would like a go at her too.

Men like me tend to stick together, to share, if the opportunity arises. I know that the eight years I've been gone will not have taken that comradery away.

It's not a really organized group and we have no rules. It's really just fourteen men, maybe a few more or less by the time I get in contact, the number is always fluctuating, who share in the same types of 'hobbies'. When one of us brings a conquest back to

share, it is usually crème of the crop type shit. Like a limber little gymnast, we could contort until her joints break.

Fuck. That would be real fun.

"You leave her the fuck alone," mom shouts at me.

"Shut up," I say back at her for interrupting my fantasy.

I'm feeling so tired suddenly, the long day has caught up with me. But I can't really end the game after only one round, so I stick with it. Heading back over to the first girl, I make a selection, and am very close to raping her with it, when I become distracted– as have the ladies.

They're all looking at the shadows on the wall, beautiful colors spring to life from the stained-glass window on the opposite side. They're shifting and dancing as the sun falls in the sky low enough to hit it. We all watch until it stops, the sun is gone and so are the colors, the shadows of the staircase blacken and morph into a shape.

"Daddy," the girls cry out.

What the fuck?

It's no longer a shadow, I watch until a form takes solid shape, going from grey and black to a man wearing a red plaid shirt and dirty jeans. The sound that comes from its direction, as he notices his family naked and raped, is that of a wild animal, he roars in anger so loud it shakes the walls of the house–rumbling aftershocks follow.

I have no idea what to do; I am frozen in shock that manifests as fear moments later as he rushes forward. His fists are huge, and as he rains them down on my body, I feel all his strength behind each hit.

My body crumples to the floor, and still he pounds. Harder and harder it feels, faster and faster they come. Then, I see from the corner of my bloodied eye, him draw his arm back and the last thing I feel is his fist plow into my face, crunching the bones that protect my brain and pushing into it. I don't feel anything after that.

Chapter 5

I wake up feeling groggy and sore, not altogether alert. I feel myself coming back, piece by piece I feel my body coming together, it feels like my whole body has those sleep needles, it hurts so much. I feel my face, preparing for the worst. I know that

man did a number on me. But my face is fine, it doesn't hurt like I think it will. In fact, after a few more minutes, nothing physically hurts at all.

I can't help but remember the pain of being pounded on, I can feel it deep in my core. My bones remember being crushed and broken, my face knows it caved in, but I'm here and I'm healed– which makes no fucking sense.

My swollen eyes are finally able to open, and when they do, I see him here, hovering over me. I'm on the floor by the door I came through after breaking the window. I try to stand, but he doesn't let me.

"Welcome back," he says in the most sinister tone.

"What the fuck is going on?" I ask, not really thinking he will answer, but he does.

"Every night, I get you again."

"Uh, you might want to clarify what you mean by that." I've been locked up for enough years to know you don't back down or show fear to another

man, especially when he is hovering over you menacingly.

"Well, every night at dusk, you get to come back, and I get you until midnight."

"I don't think that is how it going to go down." I scramble away and reach the handle of the door without him stopping me. I'm able to get it open quickly and I dart out of the house, running as fast as my feet will take me. Only, when I make my exit, it's actually my entrance, and I'm right back in the house, stumbling forward into him, his big arms wrap around me.

"I told you, every. night. you. are. mine." He grabs hold of me tighter, pushing his forehead against mine. "That's how this works. You die, and if you have someone here who wants you bad enough, you get to return to them from dusk until midnight every night, it can be love or hate that keeps you here– one man's heaven is another man's hell. Welcome to hell, fucker. Let the games begin."

Chapter 6

He grabs me by my hair and whips me into the living room, I can do nothing against him, his strength is insurmountable. I go where he takes me, and no matter how hard I fight, I am no match for him.

He pushes me to the ground and I struggle to get free to no avail. He pounces on me and pummels me with his fists, the pain I felt last time he had done this to me comes back and I feel it stronger now. Each blow compounds and sends excruciating pain throughout my body. I black out before I know it.

***

I thought I had blacked out; turns out, he beat me until I died again. He caved in my skull and ruptured some vital organs; I know that for certain, as I feel it in my regenerating body. The pain sits in the back of my mind. I recall every moment he tormented me, even after I was gone; his fists flew at me.

I regretfully open my eyes now, it's dusk, I know, because I'm back. And of course he is standing nearby… waiting.

He must have the hang of this death thing better than I do, I don't know how long he has been dead, but he seems to have a good grasp on it. Either that, or him not being beaten over and over and having to recover from it eases the arrival. I don't

think I'll ever get a chance to know, as I don't see my circumstances changing any time soon.

I try to get ahead of him today, pulling to my feet quickly and running. Knowing the door to the outside will not be an exit for me, I run as fast as I can to the downstairs room I raped his daughter in and slam the door shut behind me, pushing my weight against it.

He turns the handle and I hold tight, then I am shoved all the way across the room into the opposite wall. My forehead slams hard into the sheetrock. I'm stunned, but recover quickly enough to scramble to my feet, hopefully this time I can go down with a fight.

I put my hands up to defend myself, but he pulls something from behind his back that is no match for my fists. He throws the knife with expert precision, it hits me in the chest, the wind is knocked out of me from the force, and my breathing is coming out with a strangled wheeze. I can't get enough air into my lungs. I choke and cough until it's all gone,

then I take my last gasping breath before all the light fades from my sight.

***

Oh, fuck. I feel myself waking again, my lungs are sore and it's hard to breathe. I lie here, instead of moving, knowing he is with me already, waiting to attack.

He reaches over and grabs me; my eyes fly open just in time to see him hitting me in the face with a meat tenderizer.

"I'm going to make this one quick; I have to tend to my girls."

I just now realize they hadn't been around, too busy trying to plan my next move to notice.

"I bet they need time to heal from what I did to them. I raped your little girls right here in this…" my words abruptly halt as soon as I am struck again by the meat mallet.

***

More days go by, weeks possibly, each one has him rushing through and killing me quickly, wanting to spend as much time with his family as he can I'm sure. I thought it was as bad as it could get. Torturing me and killing me over and over countless times.

It must have been months before I saw one of the girls. The first girl, the one I met in the kitchen, has gotten back on her feet first, joining dear old dad in the torture, she yells at me and tells me she hates me, hits me, stabs me. He stands by watching as she takes her vengeance. She's pretty tough, although he restrains me when it comes time for her turns.

A few more weeks and I see mom limp in. "Oh, you're looking a little worse for wear. You must still be recovering from the fucking I gave you, or have you always walked like you just got off a horse?" I taunt her, knowing I'm fucked either way, maybe if I piss her off enough, she will attack me quickly and it can be over. That is, until I have to do all of this shit again tomorrow.

I get so furious at that thought. I have to repeat this endlessly until who the fuck knows, trapped in this eternal fucking loop of hell. I'm not saying I wouldn't do it all exactly the same way– I had a damn good last hooray, but I would have left when that bitch told me her husband was coming. That's for damn sure.

Mom just looks at me, no anger in her face, it looks as though she might have a secret, a small sideways smirk appears across her mouth and it scares the shit out of me. I've seen a lot of things, I've never once seen a woman look more menacing than her huge ass, 'otherworldly' husband standing just next to her.

I step back without telling my feet to move, they're definitely on the same page as my brain, except that my brain can't talk right now.

"Honey, will you go get Eliza, I want her to be here for this." She kisses him sweetly on the cheek before he goes. I haven't seen her yet, I fucked my gymnast pretty good, she's probably needed the most time to recover.

"Don't start without me," he says.

"I wouldn't dare."

I fucking run, I head in the direction that always seems to be my first instinct and I'm distraught when I see the door still gone from the hinges of the room. I cower in the corner for nothing else to do and bury my face in my shaking hands. I really thought the worst was behind me. Being pounded until my bones broke and splintered, having my face caved in, is nothing compared to what this woman has in store for me.

She has a plan, I saw it in her eyes, and it isn't going to be quick like hubby. At least with him I could go back to the nothing, even if the time did move so fast that it felt like no time passed before I was waking again.

If the torture lasted longer though... I don't want to think about it. I close my eyes tight to focus on my surroundings, listening and waiting. I just fucking wait!

Chapter 7

I hear the footsteps coming closer, the thudding of the large man as he approaches. He effortlessly drags me from my hiding spot and takes me into the kitchen, lifting me as if I weigh nothing,

and setting me on the butcher- block- island counter top.

He takes my clothes off, and the smallest girl, my *favorite* girl, comes over to assist, but not with the unwrapping part– I wouldn't have minded that one bit– I am hardly able to keep my boner at bay with her around.

Instead, she takes tape and affixes it to my mouth, wrapping circles around my head and over my ears. Before she can cover my eyes, I see a contraption sitting off to the side. I know what it is right away; I just can't imagine what it could be used for in the kitchen.

Before I can wrap my head around the implications, tape covers my eyes. I can't see the rest, but I feel the very second someone has cut deeply into my thigh.

I hear the muffled voices of them all as they are talking through the next part. I hear the loud motor start and I scramble to get away.

Then the next piece of tape covers my nose and I can't breathe, which I think would the worst thing to happen tonight if I hadn't seen what I saw.

I feel the sharp, cool, metal object pushing into the hole in my leg, the noise gets louder and I hear the air compressor working, the rumble of the motor reverberates across my body.

My skin peels away, I can feel it separate, all my nerves are on fire, and although it only takes a few seconds, it's more pain than I have ever felt, every part of my body is alive and in pain.

***

I wake the next time still screaming and writhing.

The memory of being skinned alive is more than I can handle, I relive the feel of my skin balloon again and fill the gap between my flesh and bones as it separates. And my god, it is the worst thing to experience, but having to remember it in the depths of my bones is too much for me, I open my tear- filled

eyes only to meet hers again, and I can't take it, I just know this is going to hurt.

Thank you for reading! I hope you enjoyed it.

Also, kinda hope you didn't, this is disgusting.

☺